An Incomplete Catalog of Disappearance

"A monarch of the short form, Diana Oropeza has achieved the seemingly impossible: she has pulled a Jorge Luis Borges rabbit from a lexical hat. Rooted and anchored in research and fictive veracity, she intentionally confiscates academic surrealism with wit and pith. With each piece, Oropeza, much like Dorothy Dietrich catching a narrative bullet with her mouth, bends time and collapses stars, surprising the reader with every twist and turn of phrase, and bestowing phantom limbs to their chiropteran and lagomorph thoughts. These mesmerizing stories in *An Incomplete Catalog of Disappearance* hold people, (meta) things, and nonexistent beings hostage with their concise economy, whimsical non-linearity, and highly imaginative, nomadic narratives. Her work is the most electrifying text I have read in such a long time."

—**VI KHI NAO**, author of *The Italy Letters*

"Diana Oropeza's *An Incomplete Catalog of Disappearance* is a marvel. Suspend your logic, allow yourself to be pulled into the labyrinth, trust "a certain unfocusing of the eyes," and you'll be fascinated by what, gently and quietly, appears through the blur. I already can't wait for Diana's future books."

—**POUPEH MISSAGHI**, author of *Sound Museum*

An Incomplete Catalog
of Disappearance

By Diana Oropeza

Future Tense Books

Portland, Oregon

AN INCOMPLETE CATALOG OF DISAPPEARANCE

By Diana Oropeza

ISBN 978-1-892061-99-7

Cover design and layout by Jason Gabbert
Cover art by Kevin Sampsell, collage on wood panel

First edition. Printed in the United States of America.
Published by Future Tense Books. Portland, Oregon
www.futuretensebooks.com

"A classic example is the doorway which survived so long as it was visited by a beggar and disappeared at his death. At times some birds, a horse, have saved the ruins of an amphitheater."

BORGES, 1940

URGENT

What you are holding in your hands is a cardboard box. Inside the box you will find the document you are currently reading, which says: THIS BOX IS HEAVY BECAUSE IT IS FULL OF HOLES. This message will self-destruct in three, two, one

COPPERFIELD

It was enchanting—we'd never seen a statue of liberty disappear
the way this one did. A large curtain went up, blocking the
statue from view, and when the curtain fell, everyone gasped
as searchlights passed through the empty space that had been
occupied just moments before. I began to feel motion-sick, so
I asked the person next to me if it was normal to feel queasy
at this kind of thing, but they ignored me because the curtain
was rising again. And when the curtain fell for the second
time, again everyone gasped–liberty had been restored! The
searchlights became spotlights and the audience was on their
feet as the Illusionist stepped out to take a bow. When the
cheers finally died down, the Illusionist said there was no
need for applause because his attempt to disappear liberty
had been a failure, because liberty could never disappear. He
said he knew it would be a failure, but he thought that if we
could just face the emptiness, we might realize how fragile
our freedom was. Then the Illusionist slipped through a portal
that was built into the stage and disappeared. I was having
horrible mouth sweats, my inner ear was sensing something
different than my eyes were seeing, but no one seemed to
notice I was turning green; they were too busy oohing and
applauding. Doctors told me later that I must have had some
kind of adverse reaction to the spectacle, but I swear I felt the
ground move. I wanted to know more about the disappearing act, I wanted to understand its mechanisms and effects.
Unfortunately, all I learned was that the Illusionist had chis-
eled all of his secrets onto nickel plates and mailed them to
the moon to become part of some new lunar library. I just read
that for his next act, the Illusionist plans to vanish the moon

LÓPEZ

He disappeared twice. The first time was during The Process, when they placed him in a Disappearing Box for three years. One day he reappeared, though there were no doves, and for thirty years he did not speak about what happened during the time that he was missing. The day finally came for him to testify, so he began to speak, and as he spoke, everyone in the room began to levitate. But just before he gave his final word, he disappeared again. This time he did not reappear, and some of us were left still floating. Justice proceeded without him, and "Never Again" became a national slogan. Or was it a promise? A gag. The Endless Handkerchief

RAPHAEL

The subject of the missing painting is unidentified, though many believe it to be a self-portrait. Although the painting was never recovered, it has been known for years that the painting survived the war and it is not believed lost, but stolen. All the surviving photographs of this work are in black and white, so there is no way of knowing the piece's true colors, and any color renderings you may have seen have only been imagined. The painting was last seen in the hands of a military unit named The Hellfish, who stole the painting during a raid and stashed it in a strongbox at the bottom of a lake. A contract was made, a tontine rather, in which the last surviving member of the Hellfish would inherit the painting and all of its wealth. And after a series of assassinations, one sole member remained. The trunk was fished out, but when the last Hellfish opened it, there was nothing inside except a cartoon version of the portrait. Some experts believe this cartoon is the most accurate color rendering we have seen to date. As for the original painting, it has yet to resurface. The National Museum is offering $100 million dollars for the missing painting's safe return. Currently, the Museum exhibits the missing painting's original frame, empty, awaiting the painting's homecoming

CALLE

An artist hired me to follow her around in order to prove that she existed. So I took photographs of her and wrote logs of her daily activities as she pretended to be unaware of my watchful eye. I collected her existence into a manila folder and mailed it to the artist who then published it as a collection called *The Shadow*. I started following her career after that, and she began playing detective herself, following people around in search of art. She eventually began to investigate the disappearance of D, a woman who told the artist she wanted to be just like her and then mysteriously disappeared in a fire. The artist went looking for D, but never found any trace of her, though she took photographs of the ashes and published them as a collection of art titled *D*. I have never seen this work, but I originally found the artist through an author named D, unrelated, who mentions *D* in a book about flexible realities. And while there are traces, I have been unable to prove that any of this exists, let alone find a hard copy

DICTIONARY

The ceiling had caved in on the history section of the library, so the timeline was an absolute mess. When I arrived, the librarians were sifting through the ruins, trying to make sense of what had happened. One of the librarians was practically in tears. She couldn't locate the written history of the unending war, and another librarian tried to soothe her with classics. Everything was in disarray, and on any other day I might have tried to help, but today I was here for an important meeting. It was with a woman called The Dictionary who was rumored to have read every book in the library and who had a ferocious appetite for unpublished books. She was helping me translate the work of an author who needed to remain anonymous to protect them from danger. When I found her, she was sitting at a table in the darkest corner of the room, unbothered by the kerfuffle going on around her. In fact, an entire chunk of plaster ceiling had fallen 6 inches to the right of her right hand, and she hardly flinched. As I approached, I saw that she was reading a book about caterpillars, and for some reason, she was reading it in reverse. I sat down in the seat in front of her and set my briefcase down. She did not look up but began speaking immediately. "Do you know much about parasitic butterflies?" She didn't pause to hear my response before she continued. "One species makes its children smell like ants, and because the ants are blind, they accept the intruder into their home as one of its own. This allows the intruder to go undetected as it quietly devours the entire colony." I said I didn't know. She continued, "We see butterflies and we think, how beautiful! How masterful! but the truth is caterpillars just gorge, and butterflies just fuck and pillage, and it's the ants who end up burying the dead." Neither of us spoke for a moment. Then the Dictionary sighed and she reached into her bag to pull out a small red notebook. She said, "I did everything I could to conceal the author's identity, which you know wasn't easy because they left a lot of fingerprints. I took all the information from the author and rewrote the entire thing in my own voice. That way, anyone looking for the author would only find me pretending to be them. I thought this could throw off the scent." I smiled and thanked her for her work as I placed the notebook into my briefcase. She went back to her reading and I made my exit, carefully stepping over the jumbled history of the world on the way out

(IMAGE)

Old photograph, destroyed slightly, who is the subject

IMPACTO

Tonight, on television, we watch as a woman cries tears of glass. We watch as a man finds his twin brother inside of his stomach. We see the second coming of saints on a burnt piece of toast. We gather to watch the reconstruction of the host's face in real time. Tomorrow, I will look for the detective who investigated that unsolved case about the two famous artists. The one who explored every possible angle with such an obsession that he even implicated himself in the crimes, though I can't remember now who told me this. The damn satellite dish fuzzes out

BERMUDA

The Triangle is not real, although it is mappable. It is not a place, it is just an urban legend. Though it is true that many ships and aircrafts have gone missing here, which is to say nowhere, the circumstances are not always as mysterious as suggested, though it is true that much remains unknown. We may think it is easier to grapple with mystery, as if our pain was not always the answer, as if our grief was not a dagger made of ice. But of course we can't always keep track of what's gone missing, even when we know the names of those lost. Remember the Cyclops? See, most of these losses are incalculable, although it is true that there are just as many vanishings in this non-place as there are anywhere else in the world. See, we are inventing giant squid though they exist

PAULIDES

X is a former police officer best known for his extensive research on the existence of Bigfoot. For X, the biped is more than a myth, and he has dedicated his life to developing scientific proof that Bigfoot truly exists. Of course, many have ridiculed X's persistent belief but this has not deterred his rigorous search for the missing link. One day, while searching through the woods, X finds something strange buried in the ground. What he unearths turns out to be a trunk full of investigation files, mostly open cases of people who have disappeared in National Parks. X attempts to return the case files to the Parks Department, but their legal team says that the Department does not keep any record of disappearances, so there is no way that the files could be theirs. When X questions the logic of not keeping these records, the team replies that they rely on the "institutional memory" of their employees to keep track of all the disappearances. Otherwise, they say, the files just pile up. So X takes the unclaimed trunk home with him, overturns its contents onto his desk, and begins following the footprints

BRYAN

I sometimes have trouble with tenses. I have trouble remembering if I was in the present or the past or the future perfect when that happened. When C disappeared, everyone said (would say?) the present tense is more optimistic, so I tried to keep it positive: she *is* missing, she *is* lost in the woods, we think, she *isn't* the type to just disappear. Of course, it's ok to use past tense sometimes and not be pessimistic because I can say she *was* last seen, because it's not she *is* last seen, because that complicates timelines. And when she was found, she was (...is?) dead. She was (...and/ or is?) gone. In the photo on her missing persons flier, she is sitting in the front seat of her car, which is the last place she ever was. Her memory lives on while the tenses wobble

PFEILSTORCH

For years, people believed in the disappearance of birds. They would mourn them every winter until someone discovered that the birds weren't dying, they were just becoming other creatures. This was proven when someone saw a buffalo transform into a swarm of bees, and reproven when someone saw a piece of food on the floor transform into a mouse. For centuries, the greatest minds thought birds could morph into humans, plants, and even ships until new discoveries were made, and then we believed that birds were flying to the moon for the winter. And then we were taught to believe that birds were hibernating at the bottom of the ocean. It took the appearance of a stork flying with a spear through its body for anyone to realize what might actually be happening. The story of migration is so unbelievable, a miracle in fact, that almost no one considered it a possibility. And while we've studied migratory patterns, we can never understand their movement because there isn't a language for it, because the more we know, the more we become unfixed

PRINCIPALIS

I have never seen woodpeckers, I have only heard their persistent song because when I run outside to catch them they are always gone, the holes the only proof they were ever there

(IMAGE)

This image contains 200 hidden objects. Can you find them

SUFFUSUS

The same day that my grandmother's leg was amputated, I fell down the stairs. Maybe I had tried to step on her phantom limb, or our legs left us at the same time, but the doctor said my injury may have been passed down from the war. He said that, aside from my external wounds, I was exhibiting symptoms of elevation sickness and snow blindness, despite being a desert blood type, and when he ran the diagnostics report, it confirmed that I had a severe case of displacement, which had caused parts of my body to spontaneously dislocate. I explained that pieces of my family had been scattered across deserts, so it's possible we were predisposed to this kind of molting. I asked him what happens to a scorpion who is unexpectedly born on a glacier, medically speaking of course. I asked him why, whenever I saw my grandmother (which wasn't often) she would hold my face in her hands as though she were trying to memorize my face. The doctor didn't say much, just scribbled something onto my chart, but he did prescribe me a bit of venom to make my blood feel more at home. He assured me that my leg would grow back over time

DELLA PORTA

The more you apply logic to this, the more frustrating it becomes. See, it takes a certain unfocusing of the eyes to see the hidden pictures. Some things are unrecognizable until they are viewed properly, so it works best if you can go a bit cross-eyed, or wall-eyed. The idea is to blur two similar but not identical images together. This allows you to see in dimension and in depth, like the famous optical wallpaper. Although it is considered a new way of looking, it isn't harmful. Actually it's been proven that your eyesight gets better in a very short time. Just look at the legendary cryptographer, a.k.a the Professor of Secrets, who was able to read one page of his book with one eye and the other page with the other eye. Since the Professor's right eye was able to read the future, many thought him to be an occultist. Given that many of his peers were imprisoned for their future thinking, he had to find more discreet ways to share his visions. So the Professor bought a dozen eggs, boiled them, and wrote on their shells in invisible ink, and only when the egg was cracked would the message appear, inscribed in the egg white. He delivered these messages to the prisons himself, where the eggs went unchecked by guards, their ordinariness was as a kind of camouflage, a kind of hidden dimension, containing a message meant to be eaten upon reading. Now do you see it

WALLY/WALDO

Someone once pretended to be Werner Herzog reading a Where's Waldo? Speaking in Herzog's voice, they said "perhaps Waldo doesn't want to be found. Perhaps Waldo wants to be lost in crowds, free and undetected." Of course, no one could know for certain what the fictional Waldo was experiencing. As far as we know, Waldo was born in Britain under the name Wally and only changed it to Waldo when he moved to North America. We know that the real Herzog is German, but he refers to Wally as Waldo because his impersonator is American. We also know that there are events taking place worldwide where thousands of participants dress in stripes and play Hide-and-Seek. Just as we know these people are not the real Wally/Waldo, we know that this is not the real Herzog speaking. Someone is pretending to be someone reading a book with no words about someone who may or may not be in the process of disappearing. In Herzog's voice, someone asks, "In searching for Waldo, did we find ourselves

AKBAR

I found myself speaking inside a poem of Akbar's, speaking of an atomized absence, speaking of ants carrying home the names of new colors. His words were both of us. My tongue too was born in books, the stories were ours/our own, my mouth a multiplication of Akbars, of another Akbar, who went missing inside the stomach of a python, who disappeared for two days until the python slithered into Akbar's backyard monstrously swollen. (Was he returning Akbar home?) When the locals cut the snake open, Akbar was inside, Akbar was gone. Akbar says this crayon's name is Latin for "nothing follows" or "some things are missing," which I call cetera desunt, or "a work unfinished." Our names, some trace of a dead language

DEPRONG MORI

As it is told, the ghost had bitten a child on the hand. The following day, the child shocked everyone by suddenly playing the piano like a master. The child, never having touched a piano before, now rivaled the world's greatest composers. Some hypothesized the child was simply an undiscovered genius, until the wound healed and the music stopped completely. People spoke of it for years afterward, and some even prayed for their own bite, so that they too might experience temporary brilliance. As it went, the ghost turned out to be a bat, according to researchers, and a rare one at that. And now, it sits preserved in a block of lead on exhibition at the museum, newly named after its captor. And yet, no one can account for the appearance of music. Some suggested it was a reaction from the bite, a kind of spasm or temporary fever. People would often ask the child for details but the child could only tell make-believe stories. And as time wore on, the child could no longer recall what actually happened

(IMAGE)

Strange self-portraits with the faces scrawled out, cluttered amongst scraps of news and serial mysteries, dust, and a dead spider

MILTON

The monster under my bed is Schrodinger's cat. My brother
is crying under the bed, hidden in sight because it's impossible to know if the cat has been poisoned unless you open
the box. Interpretations of this thought experiment say the
cat is simultaneously alive and dead, but when one sees the
cat, it is either alive or dead, not both alive and dead. The
bottle of grappa with flowers inside of it was not the only
souvenir I kept from my first love, but Schrodinger's cat
drank it one night and refilled the bottle with water so I
wouldn't notice. So it wasn't gone but the bottle was trans-
parent and anyone could see the flowers were without form.
It's cruel to keep a cat inside a box as an experiment, to leave
a cat in quantum space under the bed, alone in poison and
paradox. Someone please, let them out

HSBD-IRYT

After receiving an anonymous tip that the body of a famous mobster had been buried in a nearby village, excavators went to work digging. While they didn't recover the body, what they uncovered instead was a pile of bones that experts later confirmed were dodo birds. Their hooked beaks did not look the way they had been rendered in books, though they have been rendered so differently that their appearance is mostly unknown. In fact, for a long time no one even knew they existed, believing them myth until they saw the evidence. These bones were a beautiful color, one that hadn't been seen by the human eye since before the creatures went extinct. But what was the name of that primordial blue? They said it was the original color of the sky, the pigment used to paint gods. Now they say our sky is violet, our eyes just can't see it, and they say the dodos went extinct because they were fearless but flightless, and now they are nothing but bones, which we are still finding piles and piles of. I don't know how to pronounce the name of this color, the blue of desecrated bone, but I do know that a group of dodos is called an absence

TROPHALLAXIS

Where I live, it's not easy to find cow stomachs. In The Horse, where my family is from, they dangle whole carcasses in doorways and eat every part of the animal. Ants share stomachs too. They regurgitate things for others to feast on in a kind of social ritual. They will share a kiss with unknown ants, a chemical kiss made from the contents of their stomachs. And in this way, the ants can taste where each other are from. Some ants will devour anything in their path, stopping only when they no longer hear the children's cries for food. But of course this hunger is never finished. A colony of driver ants can skeletonize a horse in a matter of minutes. Maybe people don't prefer to eat stomachs because it reminds them of a kind of cannibalism, but where I was born, whole families ate each other up. And where I am from, the stomach is a shared and perpetual gnawing

SEOW & LAI

M lost her home in a scam, swindled by so-called friends, and lost all contact with her family, saying she was too ashamed to show her face. Instead, she lived on the street for five years. Her whereabouts unknown to anyone, she headed to the nation's largest city, and among many other people experiencing homelessness, she slept at a 24-hour McDonalds, which offers refuge found in few other places. M came in one day, exhausted, and curled up next to another displaced woman who made room for her on the crowded bench. The woman introduced herself to M by saying she shares a surname with the CEO of McDonald's, and they both laughed at the cruel joke. Eventually, they fall into a comfortable sleep together on the bench, their feet pointed in opposite directions, heads nearly touching. Exactly one hour later, M woke up to some kind of disturbance. There were paramedics and police officers all around her, and even the Associated Press was there taking statements. Apparently, the woman next to M had been dead for hours and had gone entirely unnoticed by diners who thought she was merely sleeping. M was confused, "But that can't be." she said, "I just spoke with her, only an hour ago. We were laughing. She made room for me." The officer on duty said that M's testimony was inconsistent with the video surveillance, but the AP took her statement, nonetheless. The following Sunday, M's son was at home reading the newspaper when he came across an interesting article about a group of people dubbed "McRefugees" who were first discovered after a woman died unnoticed and unnamed. The article included numerous images of sleeping bodies slumped in colorful booths and also included a quote from M, saying she would rather disappear than experience shame. At which point M's non put down the newspaper and flew to the golden arches to be reunited with her, because some doors never close

DÁVILA

There is a knock at the door. When I open it, there is a single, empty chair sitting on the doorstep. I don't know what this chair is doing here or who could have brought it, but it's getting rained on and I can't help but think it's important. Plus it reminds me of someone, and it's very dark out, so I bring it inside to decide what should be done with it. I do not sit in it, because I believe that there is already someone sitting in it, someone I can't see, since chairs can't knock on doors by themselves. So I pull up a second chair in front of the empty chair and wait for my guest to speak

(IMAGE)

A collection of images I saw but was not able to capture,
enlarged, printed, and framed

NOWAK

We had all led different lives in the time lapse. To be exact, one hour on earth is seven years in space. My mother was orbiting most of my life, working with robotic arms while my father was exploring the lives of coal miners buried nearly 3000 feet below ground. I spent half my time looking up and the other half looking down. How often I confused microscopes with telescopes. Fingers stretched towards the gaping and infinite universe, trying to collect evidence that connected robots back to dirt. My mother denies that she ever wore diapers. And anyways, astronauts call them Maximum Absorption Garments. She drove 900 miles without stopping, she put lightyears between us. The body requires warmth it cannot provide itself, so a family is forever in training. Sometimes a mother is a distant planet and a father is only his word. Sometimes I am a moon and other times I am the tide, my arms stretching in every direction and never touching

SWAMIGAL

The Poet/Saint locked himself in a room and left clear instructions that no one should open it. However, a few months later, the government went against his wishes and decided to enter the room. But when they opened the door, they found no one inside, no clues, nothing. One of the officials naïvely asked if it was possible that the Poet/Saint had turned into the single lightbulb that was dangling in an otherwise empty room. The rest of the officials laughed and laughed. They said a man cannot become a lightbulb, a lightbulb is man-made. They said the Poet/Saint is more than a lightbulb, he is light itself. Clearly, he has achieved transformation into the body of a Godhead who cannot be perceived by anyone. They said the official should feel very blessed to see what he had seen. The naive official nodded as though he understood the miracle, but he still had so many questions. For instance, how could he know for sure that he had witnessed an imperceivable Godhead? But of course he was too embarrassed to ask

MALUS

He says that no one eats their own apples but in this book
based on history there is an apple tree that eats its own
apples and in this story a priest says "god told me the devil
was in the apple trees" and in a book based on miracles one
woman eats an apple from her garden not realizing it's a
snake and in this book we find the phrase, "keep me as the
apple of your eye" and in French the phrase "tomber dans
les pommes" means "to fall into the apples" which means a
kind of weakness and in the legend of Newton's theory of
gravity the apple is both an assault and a discovery and in
gravity we see the interconnectedness of mass and energy
and in the apple itself is both a meal and a seed though
there is a god planting apples not meant to be eaten

HOUSEKEEPER

Fold the towels into soft animals. Wear quiet, clean shoes.
Place all signs of life into the mop bucket. Vacuum yourself
out of the room

MIRIAM

Oh, she hasn't lived here for years. The landlord told me that when she used to live in my small apartment nearly twenty years ago, she kept 300 orchids and lived alone. No, she hasn't lived here for twenty years but the letters still come, in fact more letters for her than for me. She left no forwarding address, so I can't send her any of these letters, most of which are about cremation, life insurance, and buying coffins in bulk, so it's likely that she's dying, or maybe she is already dead. I often think of her and the orchids, and every time a letter arrives, I look for traces of their perfume in my apartment. Then I write DOESN'T LIVE HERE on the letters and stuff them into the outgoing box

ECONOMY

The scorpion count had grown so high in our hometown that the government declared a state of emergency. They offered to buy every scorpion that the villagers could capture—dead or alive. Once the scorpions were hunted and captured, they were drowned in resin, sugar, or tequila. They were transformed into ashtrays and lollipops and sold to tourists who'd come to see the scorpion capital where there are fewer and fewer scorpions everyday

FLORITA

The first time the psychic appeared on television, she felt herself going into a trance. She did not want to embarrass herself in front of a national audience, but there was no way to stop a message from the spirit realm from passing through her. The psychic's eyes rolled back into her head so that only the whites could be seen, and she began speaking in a different, deeper voice. She said, "I predict a void in which the parameters of the universe switch properties." The television host smiled warmly as he inquired, "Are you speaking with someone from the Underworld now?" The host gave the camera a playful look, and the live audience tittered, but the psychic's voice only grew deeper. "...I predict a giant hole which will open up and swallow us whole." The host began to fidget in his seat as he asked, "Are you trying to tell us that there is some major disaster headed towards us? Like some kind of black hole, or spacetime singularity?" He smiled at the camera, lightly winking and rolling his eyes. The audience fell into a more comfortable laughter, until the psychic clapped in a thunderous voice: "It will swallow us whole unless we can reach the center of the abyss without gravity tearing us apart!" And then the psychic began to convulse. Suddenly, the host jumped back and out of his chair. He quickly motioned off-stage, and shrieks could be heard as the room began to buzz with a strange static. The psychic continued to violently shake, and at one point she bit through her tongue so blood began pouring from her mouth. She began to scream a pure 1 kHz tone so clear that lightbulbs started to burst. Crew members rushed on stage and grabbed the flailing psychic

by the arms in an effort to remove her. As she was being
carried off, the psychic lost transmission with the spirit
realm and suddenly came to. She realized quickly that she
was under restraint, blood staining her teeth and chin, and
in her normal voice she asked frantically, "What happened?
What did I say?!" And then the televisions cut to Test Card

FATA MORGANA

It's difficult to distinguish a mirage even if we know about thermal inversion because what we are actually seeing is the famous ship, the one that can never go home. Only, what we are seeing isn't really the ship because the ship is out of sight (and maybe never existed to begin with). See, this is not a pipe, and it is not the symbol of a pipe, it is a statement about phenomenal distortions and it is something else. Something that needs naming and fairy tales like this famous ship, doomed to sail the seven seas for eternity. A blur we named, a blur we built histories around, histories that float in air, like captains naming non-existent mountains after themselves. Or the infamous ship who looked at an iceberg and saw a false horizon. We rub our eyes and it's still there

PENG

Our expedition leader vanished after he left a note saying he had gone to get water. We were a group of biochemists looking for a flower that had never been seen before, a flower known only as "the hidden heart," a flower which supposedly had been born from the debris of nuclear testing and held the secrets to regeneration. We believed that if we could understand the flower's chemical structure and biological links, we might be able to better understand how living organisms survive inhospitable conditions, and be able to extract resilience compounds from the plant. The only problem is that the closer we came to knowing the flower's location, the further we got from understanding our own. Unfortunately, the flower was endemic to Wandering Lake, which is known for intermittently shifting its location, so it's possible that our leader went looking for water that he remembered was there, not knowing that the water had legs and walked across the desert. I like to imagine that he found the hidden heart, and didn't want to leave its side for fear he might not see it again. Maybe he's there now, hoping the rest of us find it too, the flower that can grow out of war. Only the rest of us didn't know if we should keep waiting until our expedition leader returned, but we also weren't sure of the way forward, or home

(IMAGE)

The kids in the foreground are gawking at something that can't be seen from this angle, their eyes are wide with wonder

JAMAIS VU

I awake to the sound of a string quartet inside my house
but when I go downstairs to see the strings, there are only
jet engines, and they are blowing so hard that my cheeks
pull back over my teeth. I am yelling, "What song is this?"
and they are calling out tune names in tongues. I think I
hear one say "Dream a Little Dream" and I start to sing
along and yes, it isn't Dream a Little Dream, it's actually
the piece by Sofia Gubaidulina, yes it's that song loud and
clear. Except no, there's a different song in there, or under
it, that isn't being spoken. It's not voiceless, just unnamed,
and not quite acknowledged. Or we just haven't heard it
fully. See we have always known these songs, we are just
now remembering to know them well. And the jet engine
orchestra hits a chord I've never heard yet, a gorgeous disso-
nance, all the voices playing at once

BAZAAR

I disappeared once, just for a moment. No one knows where I went, not even me. We were out of town, and we had stopped at a flea market. I wasn't even 3 years old. My mother looked away for an instant and that's when I vanished. She says she cried out my name over and over again, and everytime she tells the story, she cries out my name just like she did that day until finally I materialize out of nowhere. Now, I know I wasn't lost (though I can't actually prove it) my mother just couldn't see me, but to this day she loses sleep. In this way I am always disappearing. Where do I go and why do I keep her up at night

PATZ

My wife said she couldn't stomach these stories about missing kids as she ate her cereal; too sad for breakfast, she would say. I know that it's a lot to swallow, but from my experience, it's worse not to look. Anyway, it was my job to move these milk cartons, obviously I'm retired now, but for years I drove the forklift at the dairy factory, so I couldn't very well just close my eyes. I had to stare at these kids' faces day in and day out. Every day I'd go to work and there'd be a ten-foot-tall wall of them staring back at me. I'd load them into the delivery trucks, and the next day, there'd be a whole 'nother stack of them. Did that for about 10 years. And yeah, it hurts me to say that we never found any of them. Not that it was the responsibility of the dairy workers to find them, not that it wasn't either. The general consensus was that it didn't make sense anymore, that by the time the milk cartons circulated, the children had already been missing for weeks or even months. Which I always found strange, since milk spoils so quickly

The year of mass hysteria began when one child ate a slice of birthday cake and promptly began experiencing symptoms of demonic possession. Her eyes spun in every direction and she began to projectile vomit. The stench quickly became overwhelming, and soon all the party guests began to vomit. In a classic prisoner's dilemma, everyone at the party pointed the finger at someone else, until eventually the group turned against the baker. The baker admitted that, of course she had baked the cake, but she had only done so upon request by the party's hostesses Miss Sarah and Miss Sarah. Authorities took testimony from all the witnesses, but because the hostesses had the same name, it made it difficult for them to differentiate which Sarah was which, and it was also difficult to differentiate between what vomit was demonic and what vomit was simply reactionary. The situation was taken to the courts that same afternoon, and it was determined by a jury of townspeople that all the party guests be sentenced to death, given that it was impossible to tell who had or had not been possessed by a demon. So all the guests were taken to the gallows in their party clothes. As for the child who was initially possessed, she mysteriously disappeared. In fact, she went missing from the record nearly all together. In fact, no one knew anything about her origins or parentage to begin with. And come to think of it, we still know nothing about demons

SANDIEGO

An orphan, same name as my mother, a wise child, turned
mastermind, turned international spy, turned double agent,
turned triple agent, quadruple agent. Couldn't remember
what country she worked for, couldn't remember if she was
a protagonist or a villain, couldn't remember if she was
catching bad guys or outsmarting intelligence agencies,
couldn't remember where she'd been. Remember, she was
an escape artist, a master thief, remember she stole the
smile off the Mona Lisa, she was building a masterpiece,
remember? It was never unveiled, she was trying to show
us something, remember, she disguised it as a mystery
adventure, remember, she left clues not traces. Remember
she looked like me

RUSSELL

We are fixated on a giant foam finger, an orange foam finger that says "red herring," so no one is paying attention to the volcano erupting in the background. A teary-eyed wolf makes a film about how to disappear, starring a two-year old ghost, and the nation goes to work to find them as if they are really missing, all the while the lava flows and all the roads collapse into caves

PHEDRA

There is no myth in this, there is no record of this at all.
Why is there no photograph in this report? (Find out how
long it takes to become a skeleton

(IMAGE)

I am holding the key to the disappearing act: the woman,
she is hiding under the chair, she is folded into the wall

COOPER

A man boards a plane with a bomb in a briefcase. Mid-flight, he calls over the attendant, who happens to be my godmother, and he opens the briefcase to show her its contents. He tells her that everyone will live as long as she does exactly what he says. He tells her to remain perfectly calm and not to alarm the other passengers. They must remain unaware of the hijacking so as not to create panic. The plane will land as scheduled and when it lands, a suitcase containing a trillion dollars in unmarked bills will be brought onto the plane, along with four parachutes. The plane is to be refueled upon landing, and if all of these demands are met without incident, then the passengers, and only the passengers, will be allowed to safely exit the plane. If there are any hiccups, the man will not hesitate to press the detonator. He makes this very clear. My godmother nods and goes into the cockpit to make the necessary arrangements. When she comes back, she is smiling as if nothing is happening, and starts wheeling out the drink cart. She gives everyone a cookie like it's any other day. When the plane finally arrives at the terminal, it is my godmother who steps out onto the tarmac. An FBI agent hands her a large brown suitcase and four parachutes. She returns to the aircraft and places these items in the seat next to the man with the bomb. The man nods in approval, and she opens the door for the passengers to exit. She smiles at them and waves farewell, she thanks them on behalf of the airline. Only as the passengers begin to deplane do they realize that they were being held hostage. They are stuttering and befuddled as they are greeted by officers and reporters bombarding them with questions. My godmother closes the door to the aircraft, and the plane takes off again. Now only the flight crew remain onboard. They have been instructed to lock themselves in the cockpit and fly due North. When they feel their ears pop, they know the man has jumped. My godmother forgets his face almost immediately

MABE

It was an abstract portrait of the self, painted by a Japa nese-Brazilian artist. It wasn't meant to capture the artist's face, it was a portrait of his anguish. This portrait, along with 50 other paintings and six crew members, vanished on Flight 976 somewhere between Japan and Brazil. This portrait was not titled "immigrant song" but it might have been some translation of that. Sadly, no survivors, no wreckage, no art was ever found (see *Untitled*, and *Untitled*, and *Untitled*, and

BALLOON BOY

The hoax of course was that there was no UFO. It wasn't aliens in some flying saucer who abducted the kid, it was a hot-air balloon caught in a heavy windstorm. See, the boy and his friend wanted to go sightseeing just the two of them, so they took the balloon out at sunset without their parents' permission. They didn't know the wind would get so ugly, but soon the balloon was being thrashed around like a coin in a blender. At one point, the wind kicked the balloon down close to the ground so the friend was able to jump out, but sadly the boy was still in the basket when the wind suddenly changed directions. It yanked him backwards into the air further and further until he and the balloon disappeared behind a thick cloud. His friend had miraculously survived the fall, and he was forced to watch the boy be carried away. He reached his hands out towards the balloon as if by some miracle he might catch them. But of course he couldn't, his legs were shattered to pieces

CELESTE

As in sky, as in heaven. As in Mary, as in migration for Marie. The last dated entry in the ship's log mentioned strong winds, but according to testimony from others at sea, there were no such winds that day. Who can prove the absence of wind

LENZ

After one cyclist successfully circumnavigated the globe by bicycle, F was inspired to attempt the same feat. We gave him a big send-off, a parade and everything, and he promised to report back with what he saw. And he did. F sent us telegrams throughout his travels, recounting his adventures with pictures included. We saw the world through his eyes, we were with him all along the way as if we were riding on his pegs, together at every "impassable" road. All seemed to be going well for F at first, minus the malaria. During his illness, he wrote to us about blue dragons that eat you from the feet up, and women so beautiful they make the moon shy, though we couldn't be sure if what we were reading was truth or delirium. In his last telegram, he mentioned that he might be heading into some kind of war and would report back with what he saw. But then the correspondence suddenly stopped. After too much time had passed without a word, we began to worry about F, so another cyclist volunteered to go find him. But the cyclist did not find F. The only thing the cyclist found was F's fate. Apparently, F had insulted someone with power, possibly by accident or possibly on purpose, but either way F would never speak again, his body now part of the river. When the cyclist returned home empty-handed, we wept, we saw the world recede from us. We demanded more information. We needed to know exactly what had been said, not just for closure but for the purpose of survival. But the cyclist never found out what F had said; it had been too dangerous to ask. So I volunteered to circle the globe on my bicycle and find out

DUNBAR

Our son is lost. Our son is at home. That's not your son, it's our son! No it's not, he's ours! I think a mother would recognize her own son. I know without a shadow of a doubt that he's our son. Can you prove it? No, there is no science yet. Then you have no proof. Well, can you prove that he is yours? Yes, I gave birth to him. Well, so did I. Fine then, I am calling my lawyer. Fine with me. Who's son is this? He is ours! No he's not, he's ours! Well, the judge says this is your son. Your son is ours now. Our son is gone

(IMAGE)

An evidence board with red string and pins on maps and polaroids, clippings, receipts, plus a handful of notes that say WHY and WHAT'S THE CONNECTION

WANTED

Justice is just like blah blah blah. I wanna know what it feels
like. Is it like resurrecting the dead? Or is it like rewinding?
I am not sure because I have never actually seen it. I have
only been searching. I am seeking sources and informants.
Anyone who has ever experienced real justice please call. I
have many questions

DECEMBER

And what if we suddenly found those who were lost in December, if they became unburied like avalanches in reverse, would that be spring? And what would happen to our orbit if Neptune suddenly exploded into flowers—and is that something you can feel on earth? After all, if I am born on Neptune, I won't know that spring exists for at least five or six years and that's only if I am lucky. The day I was born is the same day the black hole was named, the same day that four of Saturn's moons were discovered, (still one hundred or more moons unfound). December is the dead season, still, we call it the most wonderful time of the year. We drown ourselves in lights and tinsel as we grapple with recurring ghosts and stuff ourselves with apples. To survive the avalanches, we cup our hands over our mouths

TROMPE L'OEIL

It's a deception. It's the recreation of the real world so
perfectly in illusions of oil that no one even bothers to
ask why the grass is now an imperial violet. And no one
seems to know when the sky turned blue apatite genuine.
Instead, we are running headfirst into walls, we are dizzy
and concussed, and unsure of what's what, you want to live
in what seems so alive, but it is slick, and you slip, and you
slip, and you slip

SSEKITOLEKO

It's practically the law around here. You can be the strongest man in the world and still not be able to live free. It's no mythology. It's no wonder that an escape plan has to start small. A brain only weighs a kilogram and a half, and with proper training, you can lift a rhinoceros over your head, and this is how you become an Olympian. Carrying the weight of your homeland on your shoulders, you travel to new lands to compete for gold. You are named "honored citizen of the world," and still the watchguards are stationed outside of your hotel. But you are light on your feet, and you manage to slip past one as he is yawning, and before his mouth shuts, you are gone. Except you don't see the lasers as you are running, and you accidentally trip the alarm. A voice booms out of the speakerphone, calling all available units, and then it begins to repeat the phrase, "Lockdown," and then the athletes are lined up and counted. Just as you are boarding a train to Japan, they find your bed empty and where your head should be, there is only a letter. In your letter, you say you don't want to return home. You say home is a struggle, so you are leaving in search of a better life, towards freedom. Just as the train starts to pull away, a robotic arm comes out of the security camera and grabs you. It stuffs you in a pneumatic bank tube labeled *traitor* and pressurizes you back

RIDER

They are holding the entire grocery store hostage. They have big guns, bazookas maybe, and they are making all the shoppers lay face down on the ground. You are working the freezer restock shift, so no one knows that you are there, quietly watching from behind a mixed medley of frozen vegetables. Directly in front of you is a comically large vintage blender with firm plastic buttons, part of a display the store is running for a summer sale to sell smoothie and margarita ingredients. None of the gunslingers' demands are being met, so one by one, the hostages are being thrown into the enormous blender. Suddenly, the freezer door opens. Someone is reaching for a bag of ice to add to this horrendous concoction, and you feel paralyzed as you lock eyes with them. Immediately, they reach their hand in and grab you , and you are yanked out of the freezer and simultaneously out of the dream. You wake up to a paramedic cutting you out of your seatbelt, and you realize that you are not in the freezer but actually you're upside down in your car. You look down and see your phone on the floor which is actually the ceiling. You look down at your hands and they are four feet long. The paramedics tell you that you've been without food or water for 8 days, trapped in a ditch not far from home. The last thing you remember is leaving your shift at the grocery store, you must have fallen asleep at the wheel. You ask why no one tried tracing your cellphone sooner. No one answers. A reporter appears and asks you how it feels to be found, and you say it's very cold

CHALLENGER

The shuttle broke apart after 73 seconds in the air. By default, the orbiter had no escape system, and unfortunately, the impact of hitting the ocean surface at terminal velocity is "too violent to survive." When we pretended to be astronauts as children, we did not simulate this disaster, even though we knew about it. Instead, we put fish bowls over our heads and pretended our mission landed safely. "Welcome home!" we would cheer, the air polluted with confetti

TRANSLATION

In Spanish, "ojos" are "eyes," but my dad hears the word "ice," which is the English word for "hielo," which is pronounced like "yellow." The word for yellow in Spanish is "amarillo," which is also the name of a place in Texas, nearly 500 miles from the Mexican border. Which translates to a seven-hour drive from home, which is actually shorter than my father's workday. At his job, he translates for the housekeepers who often don't speak English so they often don't speak to anyone except my father, except to say "housekeeping" before they knock on the door and "es clean," to let the front desk know the room es clean. The hotel staff think it's an accent causing the mispronunciation of "is" but actually "es" is Spanish for "is," so the women are not wrong, they are translating. It's just that the hotel doesn't know the verb "to be" in Spanish, which is why they hired my father in the first place, to translate between the women and staff. And of course I say women because the housekeepers are always women because even my father knows that housekeeping does not generally translate to the work of men. And whenever we drive past a "yield" sign, my father yells out, not because he is upset, but because he thinks that's what the sign is telling him to do. My eyes water, the ice melts

[UNFILED]

The shape of absence. Names become symbols that stand in for those absent. (Who said that?)

You'd think there'd be a word for that in English. A dream in which you must constantly defend yourself.

"Sharing/passing down the inability to tell a story."

As soon as anyone knew me, I was already a moon landing. I was always a chapter away.

(Note : look into species collapse.)

"Can you hear me, can you see my breath?"

(Perhaps it is not your body that we speak to, it's the wrinkle of you in space)

Where is everybody? The day is covered in ice and ice...
where are you? I am in the frosted glass. Are you there?
I am frozen stiff and all I can see for miles is ice, is ice...

(If they were there, they were neither visible nor detectable.
More importantly, nothing was there. There was nowhere
to be.)

This medicine causes amnesia.

"They said we can't do anything until we get the whole story."

(They are not talking, but they know.)

The more I think about it, the more I forget.

Remind me to ask: who is the blurry-faced person
in the foreground?

And there were two other strange clues…

Sometimes it's not a whodunit, it's a howcatchem.

But I don't pretend to know anything about shadow entities.

"In this puzzle you must find your way out of a
lose-lose situation."

(It was something about the consequences of time passing)

She was sleepwalking when they found her.

NOTES

Don't forget to include a list of everyone who ever went missing (see, public records, archives, oral histories, etc), and if possible, try to include the names of all those displaced, and if you can't find names, include a list of those missing names as well. Include not just individuals but entire populations who have disappeared, who have been forcibly disappeared. Include all their names and not just a lump sum of their remains. Carve the names of the dead into stone and place these monuments in a field of true forget-me-nots. Collect anything that has been lost along the way. Remember who said "Remember what they did to us" and hear their story

Remember to leave their families to their grief. Remember their stories too. Find a way to cope with the gravity of everything (it's easier with others.) Keep a running list of all the self-destructing evidence. Swallow a tape recorder if you have to. Make a map so large we have to live there.

BIO

At a young age, Diana developed a strange condition in which a parasitic worm replaced her tongue. The worm went on to study journalism and media at UC Berkeley and earned an MFA in creative writing from the Pacific Northwest College of Art. The worm performs spoken word in two musical projects, The Social Stomach, and CHIBI, and is also a member of Yelling Choir. In 2020, the worm self-published a poetry chapbook titled *Origin Story*. Both Diana and the worm were raised in Donner Lake.

ACKNOWLEDGMENTS

This is a work of fiction inspired by real people and events.
This is a work of journalism distorted by creative license.
This is a documentary poem.

This collection is directly inspired by: Jorge Julio López,
Courtney Bryan, Peng Jiamu, Akbar Salubrio, Mary Seow,
Ramalinga Swamigal, Julius Ssekitoleko, Phedra Walker,
Etan Patz, Frank Lenz, Bobby Dunbar, Tanya Rider,
Sophie Calle, Manabu Mabe, David Paulides, David
Copperfield, David Shields, Giambattista Della Porta,
Lucy Cooke, Kaveh Akbar, Waldo, Abigail Williams,
Kim Nowak, Mark Nowak, Carlee Russell, D.B. Cooper,
Carmen Sandiego, Roberto Bolaño, Benjamin Labatut,
Claudia Rankine, Cristina Rivera Garza, The Charley
Project, The Simpsons, Ryan Iverson, Werner Herzog,
Balloon Boy, The Challenger Space Shuttle, The Museum
of Jurassic Technology, Primer Impacto, Raphael, Miriam
Joseph, John Haskell, Daiana Kirilovsky, Jay Ponteri, Vi
Khi Nao, poupeh missaghi, Dao Strom, Alejandro de
Acosta, Jess Arndt, Kevin Sampsell, Emma Alden, TJ
Thompson, my family, the disappeared, the bereaved, and
everything and everyone that we lost.

Alas, my list of acknowledgements remains incomplete.

WORKS REFERENCED

The book's epigraph is from Jorge Luis Borges's, "Tlön, Uqbar, Orbis Tertius," in *Labyrinths*.

COPPERFIELD
Borrows and alters a phrase from an onlooker at the "Vanishing the Statue of Liberty" illusion in 1983.
References David Copperfield in a video interview with GQ Magazine in 2019.

RAPHAEL
References an episode of The Simpsons, "Raging Abe Simpson and His Grumbling Grandson in 'The Curse of the Flying Hellfish."

BERMUDA
Borrows and alters a phrase from Roberto Bolaño's, *Last Evenings on Earth*.

WALLY/WALDO
Borrows a phrase from Ryan Iverson's Youtube video, "Werner Herzog Reads Where's Waldo."

HSBD-IRYT
Borrows and alters a phrase from Benjamín Labatut's, *When We Cease To Understand the World*.

MALUS
References a story and borrows a phrase from Herta Müller's, *The Passport*.

FLORITA
Borrows and alters a scene from Roberto Bolaño's, *2666: A Novel*.
Borrows and alters a phrase from Benjamín Labatut's, *When We Cease To Understand the World*.

BIBLIOGRAPHY

Akhar, Kaveh. *Calling A Wolf A Wolf.* Alice James Books, 2017.

Bolaño, Roberto. *2666: A Novel.* Translated by Natasha Wimmer, St Martin's Press, 2009.

Bolaño, Roberto. *Last Evenings on Earth.* Translated by Chris Andrews, New Directions, 2007.

Bolaño, Roberto. *The Savage Detectives.* Translated by Natasha Wimmer, Picador, 2008.

Borges, Jorge Luis. *Labyrinths: Selected Stories & Other Writings.* New Directions, 2007.

Cooke, Lucy. *The Truth About Animals: Stoned Sloths, Lovelorn Hippos, and Other Tales from the Wild Side of Wildlife.* Basic Books, 2018.

Labatut, Benjamin. *When We Cease to Understand the World.* Translated by Adrian Nathan West, New York Review Books, 2021.

Rivera Garza, Cristina. *The Iliac Crest.* Translated by Sarah Booker, Feminist Press at the City University of New York, 2017.

Haskell, John. *I Am Not Jackson Pollock: Stories.* Picador, 2004.

Heller-Roazen, Daniel. *Absentees: On Variously Missing Persons.* Zone Books, 2021.

Müller, Herta. *The Passport.* Serpent's Tail, 2015.

Shields, David. *Reality Hunger.* Knopf, 2010.

"The Magic of David Copperfield V: Vanishing the Statue of Liberty (1983) (With Morgan Fairchild)." YouTube, @curtlow, 9 September 2012, https://www.youtube.com/watch?v=wt2JbtqF3yo. Accessed 11 July 2021.

"David Copperfield Breaks Down His Most Iconic Illusions." GQ, 17 October 2019, https://www.gq.com/video/watch/iconic-characters-da-vid-copperfield-breaks-down-his-most-illusions. Accessed 11 July 2021.

Iverson, Ryan. "Werner Herzog Reads Where's Waldo." Youtube, @ RyanIverson, 23 April 2010, https://www.youtube.com/watch?v=EvWh-6PMi9Ek. Accessed 8 August 2021.

"Raging Abe Simpson and His Grumbling Grandson in 'The Curse of the Flying Hellfish." The Simpsons, created by Matt Groening, season 7, episode 22, Gracie Films; 20th Television.

"The night time 'McRefugees' of Hong Kong." *BBC*, 27 October 2015, https://www.bbc.com/news/world-asia-china-34546807. Accessed 14 May 2022.

Bernard Maston, Donald R. Griffith and the Deprong Mori of the Tripiscum Plateau. Permanent exhibit, The Museum of Jurassic Technology, Los Angeles, CA.

Google.com, Wikipedia.org, Reddit.com, Youtube.com

Printed in the USA
CPSIA information can be obtained
at www.ICGtesting.com
CBHW020546221124
17685CB00004B/18

9 781892 061997